How to save the dragon

A book that is instrumental for teaching impulse control to children.

Author
Madeleine Matthews

Editor
Jamie McNicoll

Illustrator
Ludmila Hodis

Why this book?

Children's brains are continuously developing and during this time, they learn their most important life skills, including how to deal with emotions. Learning and growth, can only happen once the need for safety is fulfilled.

New, large and complex emotions, that arise everyday, are not a palpable thing, but are perceived and felt as a very real threat.

How can this book help?

It is easier for children to create coping strategies, when they have some practical examples to represent abstract notions. Lyrics help children remember to 'tell the story' so that they learn to process events and emotions.

How to use this book

Wrinkles represents the 'younger' more evolved part of the brain, which deals with complex processes like: planning, problem solving, impulse and emotional control. Explain to your child, that he also has such a part in their brain, and his Wrinkles part of the brain is also growing, just like them, and that it gets stronger with practice. **Encourage your child to develop impulse control.** When reading the story, and Wrinkle's presentation, discuss with your child about what it would mean in practical terms to 'hit the breaks on your muscles and heart', saying for example 'yesterday when we had to leave the park, you started screaming and throwing away your toys; what might have you done differently, if you you'd have hit the brakes on your muscles and used your words instead"?

Help your child to practice thinking about the consequences of his actions; you can use the illustration where Wrinkles is introduced. You might say to your child 'if you were to have a crystal ball that could tell you what follows after you do (a particular action) what would you see in the crystal ball'?

Flappy represents the more primitive parts of our brain that primarily deals with survival. You might find it useful to explain to your child that given his crucial role in ensuring survival, sometimes our 'Flappy', does not differentiate between an actual life threatening situation and one that 'Flappy' perceives as a threat, because one or more of their needs requires fulfillment; which is a situation that they simply don't know how to handle yet. **Red sparkle heroes** – represent the connection between a child and a parent or primary care giver. Studies show that connection between parent (or primary care giver) and child, helps develop integration between different areas of the brain;, which means that the specialized parts work together. In the book, this integration is represented as a staircase paved with hearts. **Encourage your child to remember that you are by their side**, and feeling his feelings are normal and accepted, and that the thing that needs practice is his response to the big situation.

Help your child process what happens to them, by encouraging them to think about situations that generate powerful emotions – such as a puzzle that can't easily be solved. To make it easy, remind them that Wrinkles, the wise, has the questions they need: what happened first? what made it worse? what is a name for how I feel? And that Flappy holds the pieces of the puzzle representing what happened and what his emotions were about them; and only when they work together, can the puzzle be solved. Please keep in mind that most aspects are overly simplified, so that they can be conveyed to children aged between three and seven years old.

To my son,

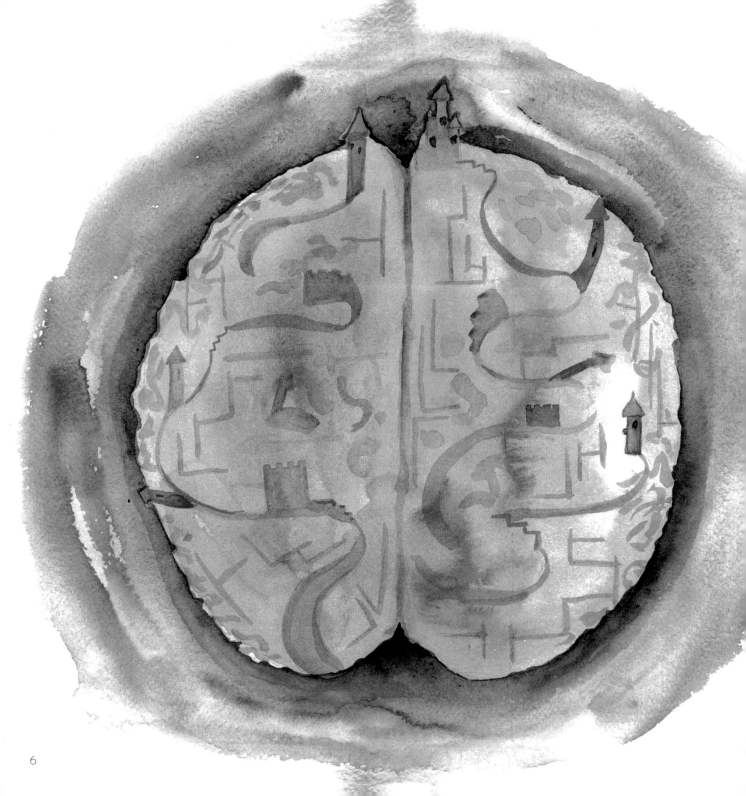

6

Once upon a time there was a land not too far away.

With stairways and forts and built as a maze

A land with no fair-princesses to save

It was filled with tough puzzles to solve every day.

Charged with solving the puzzle of the day,

Two resourceful and two cute gate-keepers hold sway:

An experienced native, a tactician and pioneer,
He was in charge when dinos spread fear.
He'll fight or flight, he'll faint or freeze,
For keeping you safe is, for him, a breeze.
He powers the muscles and has laser eyes,
His name is Flappy, on the watch at all times.

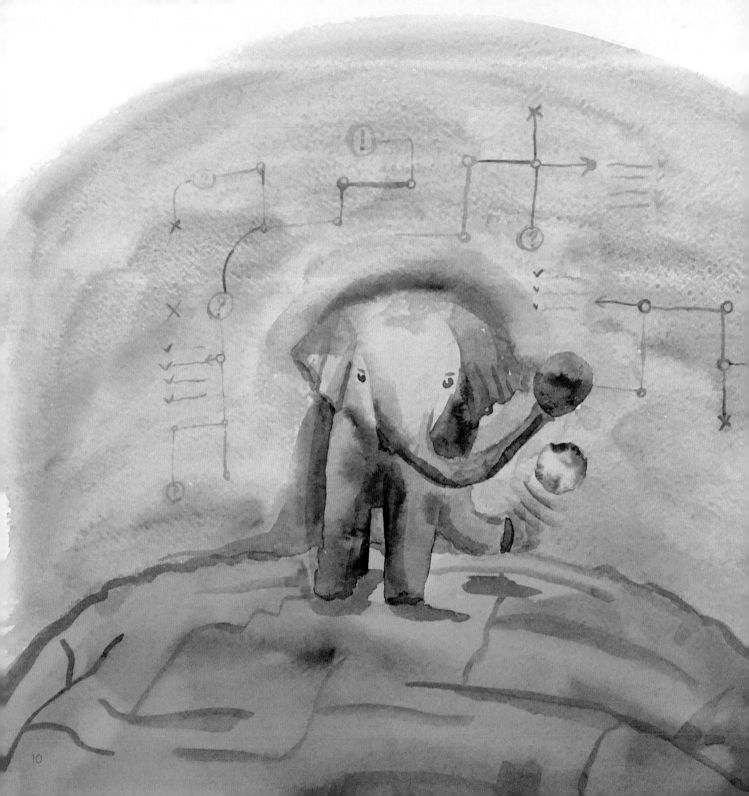

He's the new kid on the block and he loves his facts,
He pauses and thinks before he acts.
He holds the brakes for the muscles and heart,
His best friend and sidekick is the question mark.
In a crisis he ponders potential results,
Before allowing any forceful impulse.
He thinks long and hard, and acts once advised,
He's Wrinkles, and with calm his strength will arise.
Wrinkles and Flappy work best when together,
Flappy has a part and Wrinkles has another.
Solving the day's puzzle is their common mission,
Flappy brings the pieces, and Wrinkles the inquisition.

There they both were
one lovely day,
Minding their own, when they're
filled with dismay:
An alarm sounds so loudly as
out of the blue,
The light gives way to a red
pulsing hue,
Walls seem to close in, when
Flappy looks around,
And a gulf opens up where his
feet touched the ground,

Unexpectedly, Flappy is now in a pickle :
He is isolated, and cannot get to Wrinkles
But as duty calls to deal with the threat,
He jumbles the pieces, as he starts to fret.
Solving the puzzle alone?
That's such an ache!
Now, for our heroes, 'the mission's at stake.

But, as if by wonder, bubbling through,
The red sparkle heroes bring light through the hue,
They reach high and wide, stretching over the ridge,
To Wrinkles' lone floor, they build Flappy a bridge.

(F) - There's much to deal with, everything's jammed,
I cannot stop hitting with my tail and my hands.
(W) - I knew I heard something, Flappy's in trouble,
It's so tough for us when we can't reach each other!

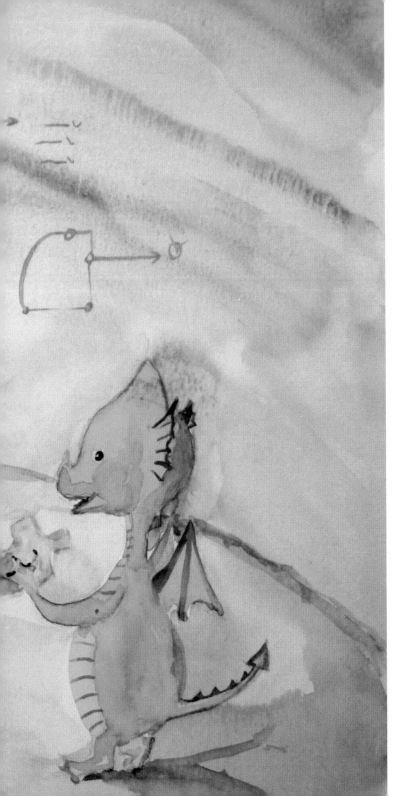

I am so, so excited
 to jump in and help,
For Flappy it must have
been tough by himself.

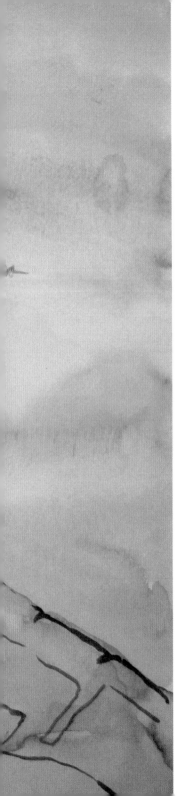

(W) - Let's take a step back and take it slow,
First please give those lungs some clean,
fresh, air flow,
You know how it feels and how bad it is,
It's locked inside you and for me it's a quiz,
When you fill in the blanks and start telling the
story,
The tensions will go and you'll feel hunky-dory.

.

(W) - Let me start the puzzle: what happened first?

(F) - My friend wouldn't play!

(W) - So, what made it worse?

(F) - He was playing with others and not me, you see?
'You're too small to play', is what they said to me.

(W) -That's when the alarm went off?
Both loud and red? Was there anything more?

(F) - I yelled at them both, and then I took their ball!

(W)- Now all the parts of the story are known
Mom says - this is - "feeling - excluded and alone".
We are so much stronger when our powers meet
So let's now enjoy that our mission's complete.

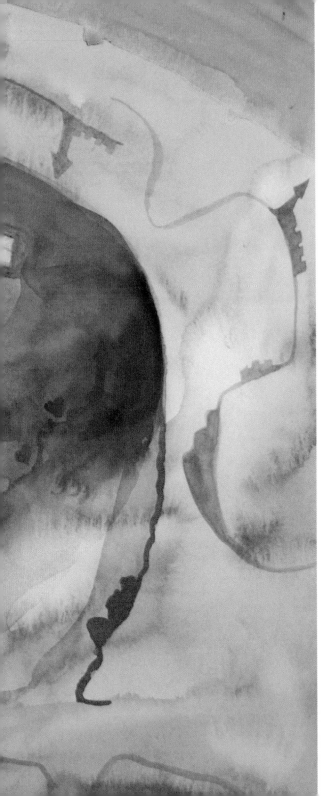

Like drowning in sorrow,
Or being as mad as a hatter,
Life's full of moments when your
mind's all a clatter.
If you remember to start telling a
fable,
You can give it a name, guess the
feeling, not brush it under the
table.
One step at a time, if you tell
the story, you'll soothe your
frustrations, you sadness or fury.
Telling the story, brings back the
calm,
Let's see what it was that set off
the alarm:
This happened first, That made it
worse,
That's what I'm feeling and it no
longer hurts.
As they feel so real,
I will pass the test,
To know my emotions,
So my actions are the best.

Fire together, wire together.

The brain grows, learns and develops based on associations. This means that if you repeat the response, for the same range of similar inputs, then the connection between the supporting neurons is strengthened. A pattern is learned.

Building ~~second~~ nature.

Following the fire together, wire together logic, we believe it is important that you and your child make time to practice brain building techniques that will contribute to maintaining emotional harmony and promote calm in your home.

The following section in our book contains four practice sheets. For each section, we've listed some prompts that may help you.

Meet your Flappy

Flappy is the more primitive part of our brain, in charge for our survival. You can spot your child's Flappy, when they respond to situations

Remember that Flappy acts in response to threats. A big emotion, such as when you feel your heart pounding and your blood boiling, is often perceived as a very real threat by a child lacking the awareness of what is happening to them & the experience in dealing with big emotions..

Flappy has three superpowers to achieve his survival goal – fight, flight and freeze.

What does 'freeze mode' look like for your child? In such situations, you may actually be wondering if he hears you at all.

What does your kid typically do during 'fight mode'?

It can be anything ranging from shouting to hitting or destroying things.

What might your child do, if he enters 'flight mode'.

Pulling away from a hug, running away?

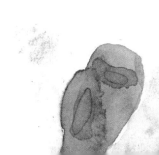

31

Some prompts:

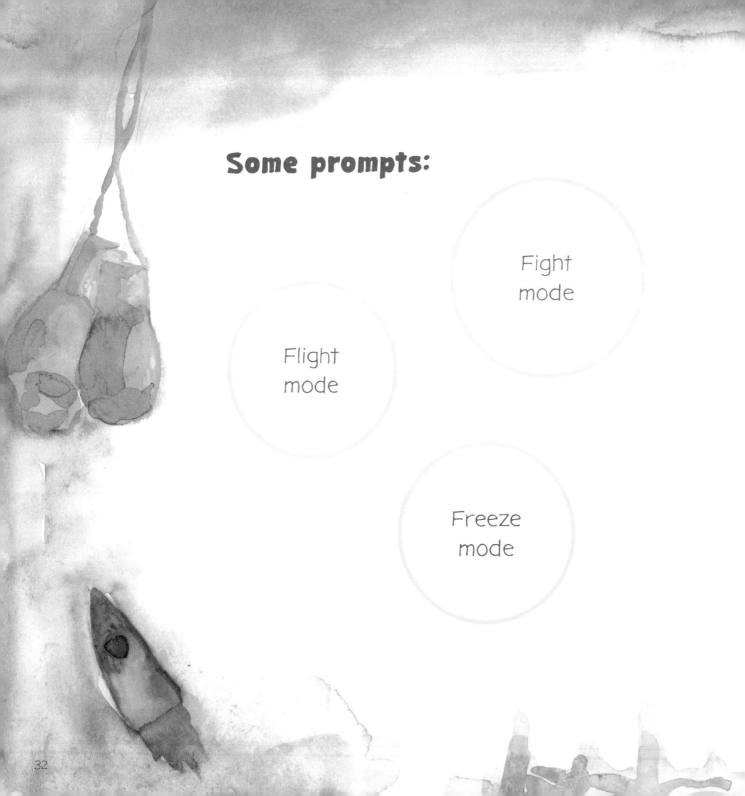

Fight mode

Flight mode

Freeze mode

Take a moment, to identify these kinds of responses.

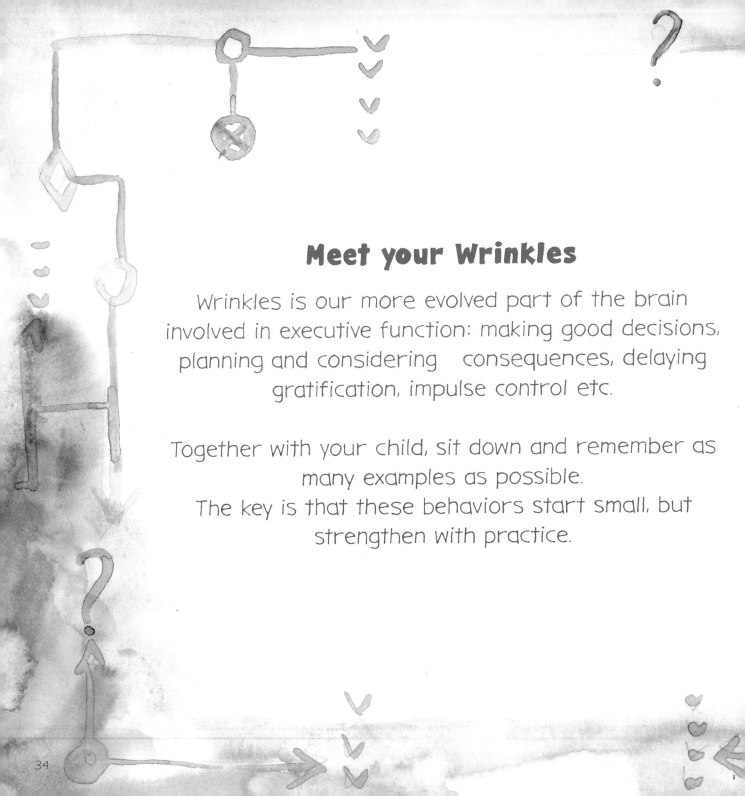

Meet your Wrinkles

Wrinkles is our more evolved part of the brain involved in executive function: making good decisions, planning and considering consequences, delaying gratification, impulse control etc.

Together with your child, sit down and remember as many examples as possible.
The key is that these behaviors start small, but strengthen with practice.

To trigger your inspiration:

He might have checked the slide, after seeing it's wet. And consider not riding it, because the speed would frighten them or their pants might get wet.

Shoes first, then run outside.

He might have pouted when you told him 'Lunch first, candy thereafter!', but he did eat the candy after lunch.

Hands washed first, then eat.

He might have used his words to ask his friends for a toy, instead of simply taking it out of their hands.

He might have used his words to tell you, he wants to stay in the park longer.

Some prompts:

Use of words not of violence

Considering consequences

Remembering the sequence of steps to accomplish tasks.

Delay gratification

Make a plan

Expressing feelings without violence

Acknowledgement is a game changer. It points out what kids do well, so they know what to repeat next time.

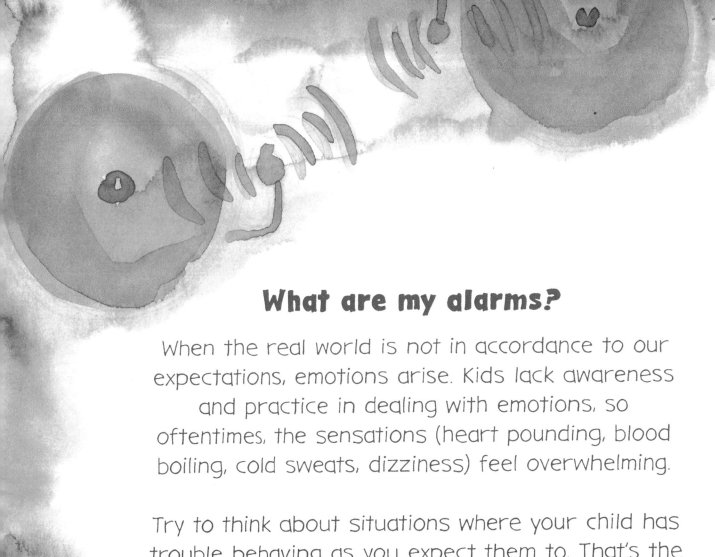

What are my alarms?

When the real world is not in accordance to our expectations, emotions arise. Kids lack awareness and practice in dealing with emotions, so oftentimes, the sensations (heart pounding, blood boiling, cold sweats, dizziness) feel overwhelming.

Try to think about situations where your child has trouble behaving as you expect them to. That's the sign posting. Those are the 'alarms'.

If you know the alarms before Flappy gets the chance to take over, you're half way there.

Some examples:

Leaving the park.

Another kid won't allow him access to a new toy.

Mom or dad leaving for work.

A kid takes away his toy.

Rushing my child out the door, and he is playing with his favorite toy.

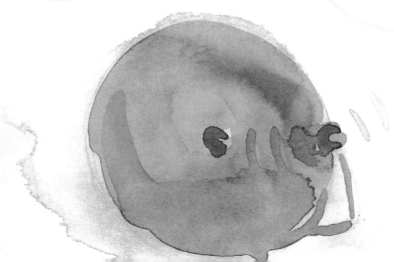

Some prompts:

Which are the situations that make your child angry?

Which are the situations that make your child shout, hit, destroy things?

Which are the situations that make your child run away?

Which are the situations that make them shut down and retire?

Working back from the examples where you child's *Flappy* is in action, identify your child's alarms.

Connection

Connection between the child and the primary caregiver strengthens the connection in the brain.
Proven research shows that your love helps Flappy and Wrinkles stay in touch and work together.

You cannot spoil your child by loving them too much.
Spoiling a child can only be achieved by:
    1) Overcompensating lack of presence/time spent together with buying toys/things/sweets.
    2) Shielding them from effort and normal frustration.
    3) Doing for them, things they are capable of doing themselves..

We love and accept our child and their emotions unconditionally. What we as parents need to do is teach appropriate behavior. That's what we practice in the other sections.

With time, you will start to notice that correcting behavior is easier when the relationship is strong. Signposting big emotions is also more frequent when they are feeling disconnected from their caregiver.

Hugs & kisses

Bedtime story

Bedtime snuggle

Sitting by their side, when they are upsett

Making eye contact, speaking in a soft voice

Watching them attentively

This sections is for identifying flags of love.

Build my puzzles. Identify, reflect and connect.

For the alarms you identified, work out the puzzle. That means helping your child identify, understand, process what happens to them. Ask yourself 'why?' and make hypothesis.

You are disappointed/angry/frustrated we are leaving the park. You would have loved for us to stay and play more. I know how fun playing in the park can be.

You love us and you wished you spend more time together. I know what missing someone feels like. Your heart hurts.

You were so curios to see how that toy looked like. It's so exciting to find new stuff/explore. It is extremely disappointing when you can't do it.

What happened first?

What happened next?

What made it worse?

What is a name for how I feel?

Alarm situation 2

What
happened
first?

What
happened
next?

What made
it worse?

What is
a name
for how
I feel?

Alarm situation 3

What
happened
first?

What
happened
next?

What made
it worse?

What is a
name for
how I feel?

Empowering Wrinkles

Now that you've identified and named the emotion, your child is more likely to be receptive to your help in redirecting his behavior toward socially acceptable, desirable, save choices to express his big feelings.

Provide information on what this preferable alternative might look like. Describe desirable actions and avoid labels like 'be good'. Ask questions and involve your child in finding these.

I would like to make it easier on you to leave the park. What do you think will help make leaving the park easier (..)?

After acknowledging their feelings, there's also the option of redirecting focus to something they may like : it is now time for dinner, playing with daddy at home.

What else might you try to convince her to share it with you?

Remember how tough it is to trust your favorite toy with someone else?

Let's come up with something that might help time pass faster, as you wait for her to be ready to share it with you?

How can we fill up your bucket of mommy /daddy love, so that it's easier on you in the morning?

Further information

Please contact the author at **madeleine@poetry.gifts** for a full bibliography that inspired us to create Flappy and Wrinkles, for an in depth explanation of the science behind these practice sheets.